# Chubby Wubbles

## My Pet Ferret

# M. J. ABRAMS

# Missing Coco

Mark put his pet ferrets, Chubby and Coco, to bed in their playpen after another long day of fun and play.

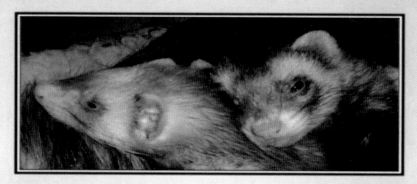

The next morning Chubby woke to find Coco missing. The door was open so he began looking in all her favorite hiding spots. He searched everywhere but couldn't find her.

Chubby wondered what happened to Coco. Would he ever see her again? "I miss her so much," he sighed tearfully.

Chubby and Coco loved each other and did everything together. They shared toys, played hide and seek in their tunnel tube, chased after each other, and wrestled playfully.

Since Coco wasn't anywhere around, Chubby rested quietly while Mark was getting dressed to go outside. Before leaving, Mark patted him on the head. Chubby wondered if Mark was going to see Coco. He was sad because he wanted to see her too. He didn't want to be left alone.

"I need to be with someone who will spend more time holding me and playing with me," Chubby thought. "I've been a good boy. I hardly ever miss my litter box because my aim is pretty good!"

Chubby thought about Mark's younger brother Jeffrey and wished he visited more often. Whenever Jeffrey came by to see Mark, he always played with Chubby and Coco. For fun Jeffrey would dangle a toy in front of them as they tried to grab it. Then he'd roll a jingle ball on the floor and watch them chase after it. They loved playing with Jeffrey.

The next day Mark surprised Jeffrey with a phone call. "Hey Jeff! Sorry I haven't called lately but I've been busy." Mark told Jeffrey that Coco was gone, and asked if he would like to adopt Chubby. "He's easy to take care of but needs attention. I can't spend enough time with him anymore."

Jeffrey was excited! "No problem Mark. I'll take good care of that cute little crumb-snatcher." Mark thanked Jeffrey happily.

# A New Beginning

Jeffrey moved out of his parents' house and was glad to be on his own. He always wanted his own pet, and now he would be sharing his new apartment with a loving ferret.

Chubby settled into his new home and looked forward to having fun with Jeffrey! It was a fresh start for both of them.

Jeffrey bought Chubby more toys and a large playpen. He kept it clean and made sure Chubby always had fresh food and water. Jeffrey gave him plenty of ferret treats as well. They were making Chubby even chubbier! Jeffrey loved Chubby and took great care of him.

Jeffrey was able to spend lots of time with Chubby every day because he worked from home. Chubby was very smart and Jeffrey taught him lots of tricks. Chubby learned to roll over, sit up, shake hands, and high five. Jeffrey also taught Chubby to come to him when he called his name.

When Chubby was out of his playpen, he liked playing with Jeffrey's shoes. He would bury his nose in them trying to squeeze inside, or drag them by the laces behind the couch.

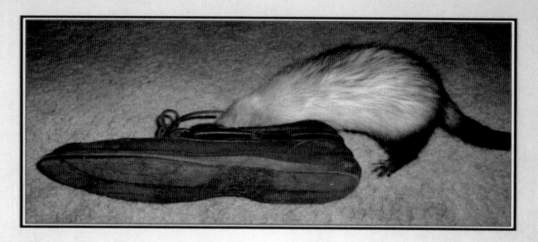

He also liked to hide anything he could find. Jeffrey always found things like pens and coins stashed in his tunnel tube.

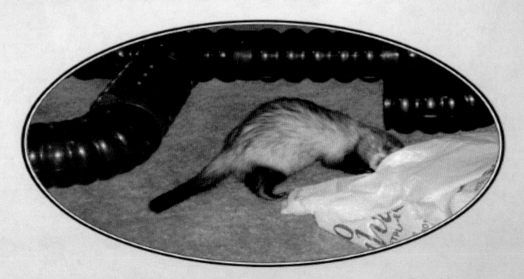

Chubby was very curious and examined all the shopping bags Jeffrey left on the floor for him. Chubby would nuzzle open a bag looking for things to play with and sometimes fall asleep inside. He slept a lot and could fall sleep anywhere.

When they played together, Jeffrey would carry Chubby in his arms, wrap him around his neck like a scarf, or drag him on a blanket. Chubby was always playful and friendly. Jeffrey had to watch his step when Chubby was out because he followed him everywhere!

One day Chubby was snooping in a closet looking for his friend Coco. Jeffrey couldn't find Chubby so he squeezed the squeaky toy and shouted playfully, "Where's my Chubby Wubbles? Where is he hiding?"

When Chubby heard the noise, he waddled out of the closet. Jeffrey lifted him up. "Are you  my little chub chub?" Chubby seemed to smile then licked Jeffrey's nose lovingly.

Jeffrey often took Chubby for a stroll in the park nearby. They enjoyed the fresh air, hearing birds chirp, and watching squirrels, rabbits, and ducks wandering around the pond.

After long walks, Chubby always stopped to take a nap. He had dreams of meeting Coco in the park, and having fun with the other animals.

# Missing Chubby

One day, Jeffrey let Chubby out of his playpen while he cleaned their apartment. As he took out the trash, Chubby followed close behind. He scurried down the porch steps just as Jeffrey closed the door. Jeffrey thought he was still inside!

Once Chubby was out of sight, he thought about all the attention Jeffrey was giving him. He loved Jeffrey but missed Coco dearly. She was his favorite playmate and best friend. "I'm sure I'll find Coco in the park waiting for me!" He didn't know why she left, but longed to be with her again.

After Jeffrey dumped the trash, he was surprised Chubby didn't greet him at the door. "He must have wandered off to sleep" he thought, as he finished cleaning.

After a while Jeffrey called out, "Where are you my little munchkin, sleeping as usual?" When Chubby didn't respond, Jeffrey began looking all over the apartment. He was starting to panic because he couldn't find Chubby anywhere.

Chubby didn't even show up when Jeffrey squeezed the squeaky toy and called out his name.

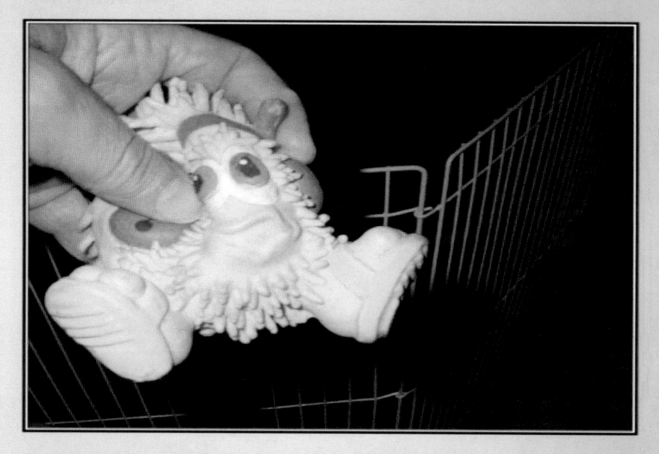

That's when Jeffrey finally decided Chubby wasn't in the apartment. He was worried and upset. "Where could he be?"

Meanwhile, Chubby roamed around the park happily. This was the first time he was ever outside by himself. He expected to find Coco and play with the other small animals. It seemed like his dreams were coming true!

As Chubby wandered along the path he noticed geese by the pond. "Wow, look at all those big birds! I'll ask them if they've seen Coco." He wanted to make new friends.

# Chubby Troubles

Back at the apartment, Jeffrey remembered the last time he saw Chubby was before he took out the trash. He figured Chubby got out somehow while the door was opened.

Jeffrey hurried outside while squeezing the squeaky toy and looking everywhere, yelling "Chubby! Chubby! Where are you?"

When Chubby heard Jeffrey calling his name, he tried to go back to him like he was taught, but it was too late! The geese saw Chubby and surrounded him. Chubby was trapped and scared!

The geese were in no mood to play. The adults were looking after their young ones. They didn't understand that Chubby only wanted to be friendly, and find Coco.

When Jeffrey got to the park, he spotted Chubby by the pond surrounded by geese. "There you are, you little rascal!" Jeffrey was so happy to find Chubby but had to rescue him!

He ran toward him as fast as he could, shouting and waving his arms wildly trying to shoo the geese away! By the time he got there the geese had already nipped Chubby before they scattered.

Chubby didn't move as Jeffrey bent down next to him.

Jeffrey gently picked him up and looked him over. "Are you okay, my little Chubby Wubbles?" As Chubby opened his eyes slowly, Jeffrey smiled and kissed his forehead.

He was happy Chubby seemed okay, "I'm sure you'll be back to normal after I clean you up."

"Those birds were biting me!" Chubby wanted to say. "I thought they would be happy to see me but they weren't friendly!" Chubby was upset that he didn't find Coco, but thankful to have a friend like Jeffrey looking after him.

Jeffrey was mad at Chubby for sneaking out, but forgave him quickly. "You could have been lost or badly hurt. You're lucky I found you when I did!" Jeffrey cradled Chubby in his arms and carried him home while smiling fondly.

Once at home, they looked at each other and thought about their friendship. Because they had a special bond they promised to always be together, never losing sight of one another ever again.

From then on Chubby tried to stay out of trouble, and Jeffrey always made sure Chubby was inside his playpen before leaving their apartment.

# Family Matters

As Chubby thought about how much he missed Coco, a tear ran down his cheek.

Chubby never gave up hope that someday he and Coco would be together again, but had no idea how that could ever happen.

A few weeks had passed, and Jeffrey decided he needed to take a vacation. His parents agreed to look after Chubby while he was away.

When Chubby arrived at Jeffrey's parent's house, he was shocked to see Coco there!

His heart was filled with joy as he ran to cuddle with her. Coco was surprised, and excited to see Chubby too! She missed him so much. They were both happy to be together again!

It turned out that Mark had to find new homes for both his ferrets. He was getting too busy at work to care for them. While Chubby stayed with his brother Jeffrey, Coco lived with his parents.

When Jeffrey returned from vacation, he thanked his parents for looking after Chubby. He packed Chubby's toys and was ready to take him home.

Just as Jeffrey was about to leave, his dad asked him if he would like to take Coco home too. "Chubby and Coco get along great, and have lots of fun playing together."

Jeffrey smiled and agreed. "I'd love to take them both home! They were meant to be with each other." The next day Jeffrey invited his brother Mark and their parents over to visit with him and his ferrets.

After Chubby and Coco finally settled in, they once again played together every day. They went on to live wonderful lives with their good friend Jeffrey, in their apartment by the park.

Made in the USA
Monee, IL
27 July 2020

# Caleb
# a
# Tyg

Dafydd Harris-Davies
Lluniau gan Dylan Williams

Dyna lle roedd Caleb yn gorwedd ar y môr llonydd wrth ochr y cei. O'i flaen roedd plant Ysgol Ger y Traeth yn gwrando arno'n egluro pa mor bwysig oedd gwisgo siaced achub, yn enwedig wrth fynd ar gychod a badau bach aer ar lan y môr.

"A rŵan dyma ein model cyntaf – yr enwog Capten Iolo," meddai Caleb.

Cerddodd Capten Iolo i fyny at ochr Caleb gan dynnu ei gôt las a dangos y siaced achub oren oedd odani. Roedd o am i'r plant weld sut i wisgo a thrin siaced achub yn gywir. Dechreuodd y Capten esbonio, "Os tynnwch chi'r llinyn yma …"

"PA-A-A-A-P! PA-A-A-A-P!"

Boddwyd llais Capten Iolo gan sŵn seiren uchel. Dychrynodd pawb am eu bywydau. Trodd Capten Iolo i weld beth oedd yn gwneud yr holl sŵn. Yno, yn dod yn agosach ac yn agosach, yn andros o gyflym, roedd Tyg.

Tyg ydi'r cwch llwyd sy'n tynnu llongau mawr i mewn i'r harbwr. Dydi o ddim yn gymeriad hoffus, credwch chi fi. A dydi ei griw fawr gwell chwaith!

"Hy! Does dim angen siaced achub arnoch chi os ydach chi'n nofwyr cryf fel Eric a finnau," broliodd Ryff, capten Tyg, gan bwyntio at gi mawr du wrth ei ochr. Roedd Eric yn sefyll ar ei ddwy droed ôl yn chwerthin am ben Capten Iolo.

Wrth i Tyg wibio heibio i Caleb o drwch pluen gwylan, fe gododd ton enfawr a siglo Caleb o un ochr i'r llall.

SBLASH! Roedd Capten Iolo wedi colli'i draed a syrthio i ganol y môr. Ond cyn pen chwinciad morlo, tynnodd y llinyn ar ei siaced achub. WWWSH!

Chwyddodd y siaced a saethodd y capten fel corcyn i wyneb y dŵr.

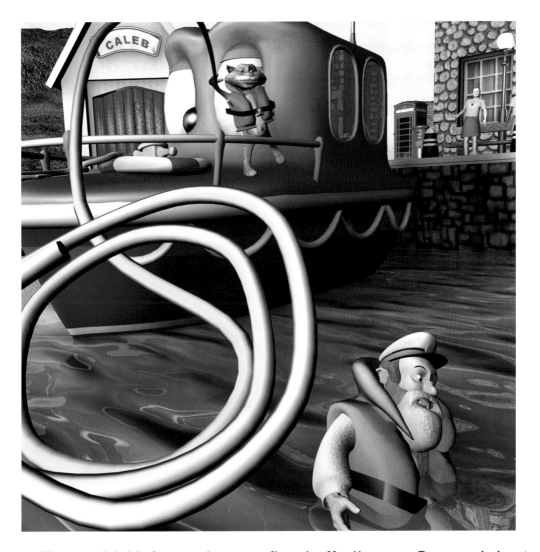

Tra oedd Haf y gath yn taflu rhaff allan at Capten Iolo, gallent glywed Tyg a Ryff ac Eric yn chwerthin dros y lle. Roedden nhw mor brysur yn gwawdio pawb welson nhw mo'r banc tywod o'u blaenau, a mynd yn hollol sownd ynddo.

Dringodd Capten Iolo yn ôl ar fwrdd Caleb.

"Ydach chi'n iawn, Capten Iolo?" holodd Caleb.

"Ydw diolch. Ond 'mod i'n wlyb domen, diolch i'r hen griw drwg 'na! Dowch i'w hachub nhw 'ta," meddai'r capten.

"Mi-aw! Dydw i ddim eisiau dim byd i'w wneud â'r criw yna, yn enwedig yr Eric 'na," meddai Haf y gath.

"Ond mae'n rhaid inni achub *pawb*, Haf," meddai Capten Iolo yn bendant.

Gan ymddiheuro i'r plant ar y cei, trodd Capten Iolo'r llyw a hwylio Caleb draw i helpu Tyg. Erbyn iddyn nhw gyrraedd, nid chwerthin ond dadlau'n ffyrnig a rhoi'r bai ar ei gilydd oedd Tyg a'i griw.

Taflodd Capten Iolo raff fawr drwchus at Tyg, a chyn bo hir roedd Caleb wedi'i dynnu'n rhydd o'r banc tywod.

Heb ddweud gair o ddiolch, hwyliodd Tyg a'i griw heibio i Caleb mewn andros o dymer ddrwg.

"Mae'n well ichi glirio'r dec 'na" rhybuddiodd Capten Iolo.

"Mae'n llanast llwyr. Bydd rhywun yn siŵr o gael damwain gas gyda'r holl raffau 'na dros y lle i gyd!"

"Does gen i ddim amser i wneud hynny – cwch gweithio ydw i – felly meindiwch eich busnes! PA-A! PA-A-P!" atebodd Tyg.

I ffwrdd â nhw gydag Eric y ci yn cysgu'n braf mewn nyth mawr o raffau ar ddec Tyg.

"Mi welais i hynna i gyd," meddai llais Guto'r Hofrennydd o'r awyr uwchben. "Mae'n hen bryd i Tyg a'i griw gallio. Edrychwch arno fo'n dangos ei hun eto, yn mynd fel siarc gwyllt am y cwch 'na."

Roedd Tyg a Ryff wedi gwylltio gymaint doedden nhw'n malio dim am beth oedd yn digwydd y tu blaen iddynt.

"O na!" gwaeddodd Guto. "Tydyn nhw'n cymryd dim sylw o'r cwch hwylio sy'n dod i'w cyfeiriad."

"Mae'n rhaid iddyn nhw," meddai Caleb. "Maen nhw'n mynd i dorri un o reolau pwysica'r môr – bod rhaid i gychod stêm neu fodur ildio bob tro i gychod hwylio!"

"Mae'n rhy hwyr!" gwaeddodd Capten Iolo, gan ganu seiren Caleb i rybuddio Tyg. "TWW-WW-WWT!"

Ar yr eiliad olaf un sylweddolodd Ryff beth oedd yn digwydd. Trodd y llyw yn sydyn, a dyna Tyg yn osgoi'r cwch hwylio o drwch pluen gwylan.

Llithrodd y pentwr blêr o raffau oddi ar y dec i mewn i'r
môr – gydag Eric y ci yn eu canol.

"Capten Iolo, mae Eric y ci wedi syrthio i'r môr!"
gwaeddodd Guto, gan hedfan ar wib at Eric, gyda Caleb yn ei
ddilyn ar ras.

"Help! Help! Helpwch ni!" gwaeddodd Tyg. "Mae'r rhaffau trwm yn tynnu Eric o dan y dŵr."

"Mae o bron â boddi!" llefodd Ryff.

Doedd dim amser i'w wastraffu. Er ei bod hi'n casáu Eric, fe gofiodd Haf y gath eiriau Capten Iolo – bod rhaid achub pawb – a dyma hi'n neidio i mewn i'r môr.

Pan gyrhaeddodd Haf Eric y ci roedd ei lygaid ar gau ac nid oedd yn symud o gwbl. Aeth hi ati'n syth i lacio'r rhaffau oedd amdano a chlymu'r lein achub Guto'r Hofrennydd am goler Eric. Cyn pen chwinciad llygad morlo roedd Guto wedi codi'r ddau i'r awyr, gan adael i'r rhaffau suddo i waelod y môr.

Yn ara' deg ac yn ofalus iawn gosododd Guto'r ddau ar fwrdd Caleb. Rhuthrodd Capten Iolo i wasgu bol Eric nes bod y dŵr yn tasgu allan o geg y ci.

Dechreuodd Eric dagu a pheswch, ac wrth i Caleb droi am adref, fe waeddodd Capten Iolo ar Tyg a Ryff, "Peidiwch â phoeni, mae Eric yn iawn!"

Canodd Tyg ei seiren mewn hapusrwydd yr holl ffordd 'nôl
at y cei.

"PA-PA-A-P! PA-PA-A-P!"

Roedd plant Ysgol Ger y Traeth yno o hyd ac roedd pobl y
pentre wedi dod lawr i'r harbwr i weld beth oedd yn gwneud
yr holl sŵn.

"Diolch yn fawr ichi am ein hachub ni," meddai Tyg a Ryff, ac fe lyfodd Eric wyneb Haf o un pen i'r llall. Ych-a-fi! Doedd Haf ddim yn hapus â hynny – ddim yn hapus o gwbl! Roedd anadl y ci yn drewi gymaint bu bron i'r gath syrthio mewn llewyg i'r llawr.

Y bore wedyn, roedd Caleb yn ôl wrth ochr y cei ar ganol egluro i blant o ysgol arall pa mor bwysig oedd gwisgo siaced

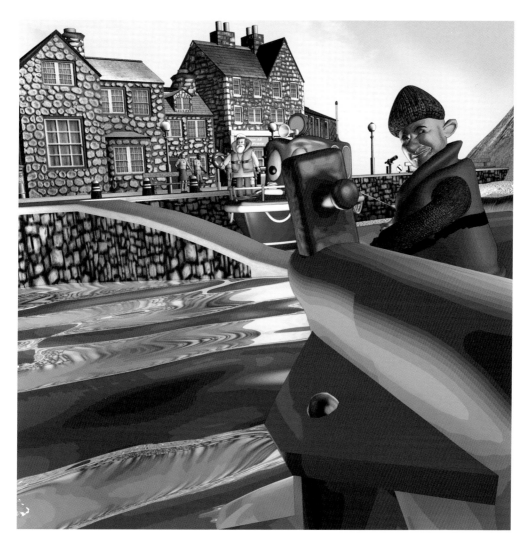

achub. Yn sydyn, canodd seiren uchel: "PA-PA-A-P! PA-PA-A-P!" A dyma Tyg yn gwibio atynt.

"O na, dim eto!" meddai Caleb a'r criw.

"Gwrandewch ar be mae Caleb yn ei ddweud, blantos," meddai Tyg. "Mae'n beryg bywyd allan ar y môr ac mae'n hawdd iawn boddi."

Syllai Caleb yn syn ar yr olygfa o'i flaen. Yn sefyll ar fwrdd Tyg, yn wên o glust i glust, ac yn gwisgo siacedi achub oren, oedd Ryff ac Eric y ci. "Gwisgwch siaced achub!" gwaeddodd y tri, fel parti cydadrodd.

Roedd Haf y gath yn hapus iawn bod Tyg a'i griw wedi bihafio'u hunain. Ond rhag ofn i Eric y ci gael ei demtio i'w llyfu eto, diflannodd Haf i grombil Caleb y Cwch Achub.

Byddwch yn falch o glywed bod Tyg a'i griw wedi newid eu hagwedd yn llwyr. Erbyn hyn, maen nhw'n griw bach hapus a charedig dros ben, ac mae ganddynt ffrindiau ym mhob man.

*Argraffiad cyntaf: Hydref 2003*

(h) *Dafydd Harris-Davies/Gwasg Carreg Gwalch*

*Rhif Llyfr Safonol Rhyngwladol:*
*0-86381-854-4*

*Lluniau: Dylan Williams*

*Cynllun clawr: Hefina Pritchard*

*Argraffwyd a chyhoeddwyd gan Wasg Carreg Gwalch,*
*12 Iard yr Orsaf, Llanrwst, Dyffryn Conwy, LL26 0EH.*
📞 *01492 642031* 📠 *01492 641502*
✉ *llyfrau@carreg-gwalch.co.uk*
*lle ar y we: www.carreg-gwalch.co.uk*